CW00549566

A S BYATT was born in 1936 and studied at Newnham College, Cambridge, Bryn Mawr College in the United States and Somerville College, Oxford. A renowned writer of fiction she has also written academic studies on Iris Murdoch, William Wordsworth, S T Coleridge, William Morris, George Eliot and others. She was awarded a CBE in 1990, a DBE in 1999 and numerous honorary doctorates including a Hon. D.Litt. from the University of Cambridge. Works of fiction include: *The Shadow of the Sun* (1964); *The Virgin in the Garden* (1978); *Still Life* (1985); *Possession: A Romance* (1990),* for which she won the Booker Prize; *Angels and Insects* (1992); *The Biographer's Tale* (2000); and *The Children's Book* (2009), whilst well-known works of non-fiction include: *Passions of the Mind: Selected Writings* (1991); *On Histories and Stories: Selected Essays* (2000) and the *Oxford Book of English Short Stories* (ed.) (1998). She was made a Fellow of University College London in 2004 and a Fellow of the British Academy in 2017.

ON THE CONJUGIAL ANGEL is the sixth in a series of Swedenborg Society pocket books. Edited by Stephen McNeilly, and drawing on miscellaneous material and other ephemera from the Swedenborg archives, the aim of the pocket book series is to make available, in printed form, lectures, interviews and other unique items that would otherwise remain unseen by a broader audience.

TITLES IN THE SERIES

On the
Conjugial Angel

On the
Conjugial Angel

A S BYATT

The Swedenborg Society
20-21 Bloomsbury Way
London
WC1A 2TH

2020

The printer's ornaments reproduced in this book are drawn from
Emanuel Swedenborg's *De Amore Conjugiali* (*Conjugial Love*),
first published in Amsterdam in 1768 and *De Ultimo Judicio*
(*The Last Judgment*), first published in London in 1758.

Editor: Stephen McNeilly

Copy Editors: James Wilson and Avery Curran

Typeset at Swedenborg House.
Printed at T J International, Padstow.
Cover and book design © Stephen McNeilly

Published by:
The Swedenborg Society
Swedenborg House
20-21 Bloomsbury Way
London WC1A 2TH

ISBN: 978-0-85448-219-1
British Library Cataloguing-in-Publication Data.
A catalogue record for this book
is available from the British Library.

Contents

Preliminary note

On the Conjugial Angel is a transcript of a talk
and reading given by A S Byatt at Swedenborg
House on Thursday 14 January 2010. The occasion
served as the inaugural lecture of the Society's
bicentenary celebrations, which featured a wide
range of exhibitions, lectures and other public
events. Introduced on the day by then-Secretary,
and former President, Richard Lines, A S Byatt
guided the audience through her novella *The
Conjugial Angel,* published as the second part of
her book *Angels and Insects*. Following this she
took questions from the floor on a range of topics
including her interest in Swedenborg, Balzac,
spiritualism and literary form.

As with previous titles in the Swedenborg Archive series, A S Byatt's response to audience questions are included and endnotes have been added. The text has been transcribed as recorded with one or two minor revisions. Passages from *The Conjugial Angel* are reprinted as published in the 2018 Vintage edition.

Readers wishing to explore A S Byatt's views on English Romantic Literature are encouraged to read: *Unruly Times: Wordsworth and Coleridge In Their Time* (1989), *Passions of the Mind: Selected Writings* (1991) and *Portraits In Fiction* (2001).

Special thanks are extended to A S Byatt for permission to print this text. Further thanks are also extended to Jacob Cartwright and Alex Murray for their work in preparing it for the press.

Stephen McNeilly (Series Editor)

On the
Conjugial Angel

I feel very nervous about speaking here tonight, being a person with no religion except profound agnosticism. But I do have an interest in religious structures and religious behaviour, and have, over the years, acquired a kind of sideways interest in Swedenborg, in particular the effect of Swedenborg's ideas on literary form. I think it has become forgotten——although it may be remembered again——just how much his ideas were present in the lives of all sorts of people.

The idea I first had was that, in some curious way, both Swedenborg's thought and the novel came out of the desire to describe an increasingly materialistic world, a world in which material science was terribly exciting, and the spiritual forms of the Christian church were increasingly coming under question. And people who were worried about fleeing Christianity, took to Swedenborgianism. And many took to writing novels, and stories, whereby the shape of the novel, from echoing the story of the Bible, began to move in a Darwinian direction: so two kinds of narrative were going on, and several of these novelists moved in a Swedenborgian direction.

I remember reading, as a student in the 1950s, an essay by Dr Leavis on Henry James —praising a book he had written—saying that the shape of James's novels might be thought to reflect Swedenborgian ideas.[1] At the end of the 1970s and the beginning of the 1980s, I used to give lectures on the James family, including Henry James, Sr—who wrote a book called *The Secret of Swedenborg*,[2] and as Emerson said 'kept it'[3]—his son William James, who was, I think, the greatest psychologist of religion ever to have written, and Henry James, who wrote two novels which I used to lecture on, one of which, *The Bostonians*, looked into all the kinds of dispersed religious events in mid-nineteenth-century America. [4]

I always think of Iris Murdoch's novel *The Time of the Angels* in which she says that the angels were let loose in heaven when God retired, and angels were let loose all over America. [5] There is a lovely quotation very early on in *The Bostonians* that reads:

> *Olive didn't go to parties; it was one of those weird meetings she was so fond of.*
>
> *'What kinds of meetings do you refer to? You speak as if it were a rendezvous of witches on the Brocken.'*
>
> *'Well, so it is; they are all witches and wizards, mediums, and spirit-rappers, and roaring radicals.'* [6]

And the mediums and spirit rappers that come through in that novel are in a sense related to the

Swedenborgian church, and *The Bostonians* is a
parodical and satirical—and on another level a
deeply moving—novel about the nature of belief.

Having given the lecture on *The Bostonians*,
I then used to move on to a lecture about Henry
James's later novel *The Golden Bowl*.[7] And this
is where I have to apologize to you, because at
the end of the 1970s I knew this novel to be a
Swedenborgian fable, and I proved it. I had all
the evidence. But it is at the bottom of Coutts
bank, with a lot of my manuscripts, and I can't
get it out. So my interest in Swedenborg moved
sideways like that.

The other writer who cared deeply about
Swedenborg—about whom I cared passionately,
and on whom I am currently working—was
Honoré de Balzac. Balzac's idea of the shape of
the novel came from his idea of the shape of
the universe, which was a Swedenborgian idea.
He felt that language was a material thing,
and that Swedenborgianism was a material
religion uniting the spiritual and the material

in the divine human. I think Balzac thought
his novels were a kind of divine human, and he
was coming along in a materialist age, writing
a human comedy, following the divine comedy.
And he said things like:

> *The only possible religion is Christianity,*
> *look at the letter written by my character*
> *in Louis Lambert where the young mystical*
> *philosopher explains, apropos the doctrine*
> *of Swedenborg, how there has never been*
> *but one religion since the beginning of the*
> *world.* [8]

Balzac was a Swedenborgian who wrote a
most wonderful novel, a Swedenborgian fable,
Séraphîta, [9] about a conjugial angel—whose
character is both male and female—who ascends
to heaven in the love of God.

So I have sat in the peripheries of Swedenborgianism, trying to work out the nature of the novel.
The Conjugial Angel, which I am now going to

read, in various parts, was written as one half of two stories in *Angels and Insects*. [10] The other half, *Morpho Eugenia*, is a fable about Darwin, a fable about Nature Study in the Victorian age. *The Conjugial Angel*, however, is a fable about Victorian religion in the nineteenth century, and it relates to the family of the Tennysons. Tennyson's magnum opus, I think, is *In Memoriam*, [11] the greatest poem of grief ever written. I don't know of anything that moves me more. He wrote it for Arthur Henry Hallam, who died at the age of twenty-two, quite suddenly. He was sitting by the fire reading with his father, when his father looked up and said something to him, and then noticed that he was dead, which was terrible.

Arthur was engaged to marry Tennyson's young sister, Emilia Tennyson, who was then nineteen. She was brought the terrible news of the death of Arthur and was expected really, by everybody——by Alfred (who couldn't get over the death of his best friend, with whom he felt somehow united like two parts of an angel), by the whole of the rest of the family, by Arthur's father who had not liked her very much but now looked after her and gave her a pension——she was expected to become a widow of a young man she hadn't seen very much of, although she loved him. But he was Alfred's friend and she was given money to be a good, chaste widow.

After about nine years of this, she quite suddenly married a sea captain——Captain Richard Jesse—— to the horror of everybody, particularly Elizabeth Barrett Browning, who said that it was in extremely bad taste and it was in even worse taste to call their first child Arthur Hallam Jesse. So Emilia got pushed out into the periphery of the family, and all that we learn about Captain Jesse, from the biographies of Tennyson, is that he could not stop talking.

And then I read, in a footnote to the letters of Arthur Henry Hallam, the most wonderful quotation from Emilia Tennyson's granddaughter, Fryn Tennyson Jesse, who became a very good writer. [12] She wrote that she had

always been told that when the elderly Jesses
had been living together in Margate, and several
of the Tennyson family had, in fact, joined the
Swedenborgian church, and had also become
spiritualists—which wasn't the same thing—
they took to having seances with the idea of
invoking the spirit of Arthur Henry Hallam, who
had been dead by then for quite a long time.

I was very interested in this, and I thought
there was a story to be written around these
episodes. I won't tell you the end of Fryn
Tennyson Jesse's anecdote about what happened
in these seances until I get there, because it is,
in a sense, the climax of my story if you don't
happen to know it. So there are real characters
in *The Conjugial Angel*, as well as imaginary
ones. I decided to invent the two mediums,
which in effect are two sides of the way I see the
presence of spiritualism, Swedenborgianism
and the narrative imagination within Victorian
life. The mediums are called Mrs Papagay and
Sophy Sheekhy.

Mrs Papagay is, in a sense, a fraudulent medium. She makes a good living by running seances, and she has a very, very vivid imagination. She really is a novelist. If she sees anybody she starts telling stories to herself about who they might be, or what they might care about. So she is quite good at it, and is performing, in some sense, a mediumistic activity in that she's reading people. Sophy Sheekhy is a very practical sort of simple, clear-minded girl, who actually does see spirits. And she sees all sorts of things, like birds and other oddities during the progress of my tale. So I will read you the beginning, which is about an angel, it is about the angel in Revelation and it takes place on the seafront, at market:

Lilias Papagay was of imagination all compact. In her profession this was a suspect, if necessary, quality, and had to be watched, had to be curbed. Sophy Sheekhy, who saw with her eyes, and heard in her ears, the unearthly visitants, was apparently more

*phlegmatic and matter-of-fact. They made
a good pair for this reason, as Mrs Papagay
had intuited they might, when her next-door
neighbour, Mrs Pope, had flown into strong
hysterics on hearing her new nursery-
governess talking to Cousin Gertrude and
her infant son Tobias, both drowned many
years ago. They were sitting at the nursery
table, Sophy Sheekhy said, and their clothes,
though perfectly fresh and dry, gave off an
odour of salt water. They wanted to know
what had become of the grandfather clock
that used to stand in the nursery corner.
Tobias had liked the way the sun and moon
followed each other with smiling faces on
its dial. Mrs Pope, who had sold the clock,
wanted to hear no more. Mrs Papagay
offered asylum to the composed little Miss
Sheekhy, who packed up her few belongings
and moved in. Mrs Papagay herself had
never progressed beyond passive writing—
admittedly voluminous—but believed Sophy*

Sheekhy might work marvels. She did from time to time astonish and amaze, though not frequently. But this parsimony itself was a guarantee of authenticity.

On one late, stormy afternoon in 1875 they were proceeding along the Front, in Margate, to take part in a séance in Mrs Jesse's parlour. Lilias Papagay, a few steps ahead, wore wine-dark silk with a flounced train and a hat heavy with darkly gleaming plumage, jet-black, emerald-shot, iridescent dragonfly blue on ultramarine, plump shoulders of headless wings with jaunty tail-feathers, like the little wings that fluttered on the hat or the heels of Hermes in old pictures. Sophy Sheekhy wore dove-coloured wool with a white collar, and carried a serviceable black umbrella.

The sun was setting on the grey water, a great dusky rose disc, the colour of a new burn-mark, in a bath of ruddy gold light poured between the bars of steely cloud, like firelight from a polished grate.

'Look,' said Lilias Papagay, waving an imperious gloved hand. 'Can't you just see the Angel? Clothed with a cloud and with a rainbow on his head, and his face as it were the sun, and his feet as pillars of fire. And in his hand a little book open.'

She saw his cloudy thews and sinews bestride the sea; she saw his hot red face and his burning feet. She knew she was straining. She desired so to see the invisible inhabitants of the sky sail about their business, and the winged air dark with plumes. She knew that that world penetrated and interpenetrated this one, grey solid Margate equally with Stonehenge and Saint Paul's. Sophy Sheekhy observed that it was indeed a spectacular sunset. One of the angel's fiery legs flared and extended, leaving momentary rosy ripples on the dull water. His swollen grey trunk bowed and twisted, wreathed with gold. 'I never tire of looking at sunsets,' said Sophy Sheekhy. She had a pale face like a full *moon, a little pitted with craters from a mild attack of pox, and shadowed here and there with freckles. She had a large brow, and a full, colourless mouth, the lips habitually lying restfully together, like the folded hands. Her lashes were long, silky, and almost invisible; her veined ears could be seen in part, under heavy wings of hay-coloured hair. She would have been unsurprised to be told that the sun and moon are constant sizes to the apprehension of the human eye, which confers on them bearable dimensions, roughly the size of a guinea coin. Whereas Mrs Papagay, with William Blake, would have divined an innumerable company of the Heavenly Host crying, 'Holy, Holy, Holy, is the Lord God Almighty.' Or with Emanuel Swedenborg, who saw great companies of celestial creatures sailing through space like flaming worlds. A gathering of angry gulls was disputing a morsel in mid-air; they rose together, screaming and beating, as*

Mrs Papagay's angel dislimned and grew
molten. His last light cast a momentary flush
across Sophy's white face. They quickened
their step. Mrs Papagay was never late. [13]

So they go into the house of Captain and Mrs Jesse,
and there is present a Swedenborgian I invented,
called Mr Hawke. This story is full of complicated
verbal jokes——there is a place in *Hamlet* where he
says he can tell 'a hawk from a handsaw'——and
the next character is called Mrs Hearnshaw, who
has lost five dead babies, one after the other, and is
trying to contact the spirits of her dead children in
the seance. And they begin by talking about whether Swedenborg's visions were caused by coffee:

Captain Jesse and Mr Hawke were both
drinking tea. Captain Jesse was speaking
about the cultivation of tea on the mountain
slopes of Ceylon, describing tea as he had
drunk it, 'aromatic and fresh-*tasting, Sir,*
like an infusion of raspberry-leaves here, tea

*transported in lead-lined caskets has always
a* musty *overlay to its taste for those who
have experienced it where it is grown, out of
simple terra-cotta bowls no bigger than this
salt-cellar, it tastes of the* earth, *Sir, and of the
sun, a true nectar.' Mr Hawke was speaking
simultaneously of Swedenborg's incessant
coffee-drinking, to the noxious effects of
which some less than glorious spirits had
ascribed his visions.*

*'For coffee, acting on a pure tempera-
ment, will they say produce excitability,
sleeplessness, abnormal activity of mind
and imagination and fantastic visions—
also loquacity. I credit these effects of coffee, I
have observed it to be so. But he is a medical
pedant who would try to pour the* Arcana *or
the* Diarium *out of a coffee pot. Nevertheless
a truth may be hidden here. God made the
world, and therefore everything in it, including, I suppose, the coffee-bush and coffee-
bean. If coffee disposes to clear-seeing, I do*

not see that the means injures the end. No doubt seers are as regular fabrics as crystals, and not a drug or berry is omitted from their build, when it is wanted. We live in a material time, Captain Jesse—apart from metaphysics, the time is gone by when any-thing is made out of nothing. If the visions are good visions, their material origin is also good, I think. Let the visions criticise the coffee and vice versa.'

'I have known hallucinations to be brought on by green tea,' replied Captain Jesse. 'We had a Lascar seaman who regularly saw demons in the rigging until he was induced by a mate to curtail the quantity he imbibed.' [14]

So we are running here between the material and the spiritual, as it were. The next passage I would like to read is the seance, where they are trying to communicate with Mrs Hearnshaw's five dead babies, all of whom she christened Amy,

and people actually did this——you can see it on
Victorian gravestones in churchyards.

*Mrs Hearnshaw was not noticing the sofa.
She was speaking her grief to Emily, to Sophy
Sheekhy, who had settled on a foot-stool near
them.*

'She seemed so strong, *you know, Mrs
Jesse, she waved her arms so lustily and
kicked with her little legs and thighs, and
her eyes saw me so quietly, all swimming
with life. My husband says I must learn not
to attach myself so to these tiny creatures
who are destined to stay with us so briefly
in time——but how can I not, it is natural,
I think? They have grown under my heart,
my dear, I have felt them stir there, with fear
and trembling.'*

*'We must believe they are angels, Mrs
Hearnshaw.'*

*'Sometimes I am able to do so. Sometimes
I imagine horrors.'*

Emily Jesse said, 'Speak what is in your mind, it will do you good. Those of us who are wounded to the quick, *you know, we suffer for all the others, we are appointed in some way to bear their grief too. We cry out* for them. *It is no shame.'*

'I give birth to death,' said Mrs Hearnshaw, speaking the thought she walked about with, constantly. She could have added, 'I am an object of horror to myself,' but forbore. The mental image of the mottled limbs, after convulsion, of the rough, musty clay bed, was always with her.

Sophy Sheekhy said, 'It is all one. Alive and dead. Like walnuts.'

She saw very clearly all the little forms, curled in little boxes, like the brown-skinned white lobes of dead nuts, and a blind point like a wormhead pushing into light and airy leafage. She often 'saw' messages. She did not know whose thoughts they were, hers or another's, or whether they came from

Outside, or whether everyone saw similar messages of their own.

They were joined by Captain Jesse and Mr Hawke.

'Walnuts?' said Captain Jesse. 'I have a great partiality for walnuts. With port wine, after dinner, they can be most tasty. I also like green, milky ones. They are said to resemble the human brain. My grandmother told how they were used in certain country remedies which might be closer to magic than to medicine. Would that be a correspondence that might interest Emanuel Swedenborg, Mr Hawke? The encephaloform walnut?'

'I do not remember having seen any animadversion on walnuts in his writings, Captain Jesse, though they are so voluminous, some reference may indeed be hidden away there. The thought of walnuts always makes me think of the English mystic, Dame Julian of Norwich, who was shewn in a vision all

that is *like a nut in her own hand, and told by God Himself, "All shall be well, and thou shalt see it thy self that all manner of thing shall be well." I think what she may have seen may have been the thought of some Angel, as it appeared in the world of Spirits or in the world of men. She may have been in a sense a precursor of our spiritual Columbus. He relates, you know, how he himself saw a beautiful bird in the hand of Sir Hans Sloane, in the Spirit World, differing in no least detail from a similar bird on earth, and yet being—it was revealed to him— none other than the affection of a certain Angel, and vanishing with the surcease of the operation of that affection. Now, it appears that the Angel, being in Heaven, would not be aware of this* indirect *forthgoing in the world of Spirits, for the angels see all in its highest Form, the Divine Human. The highest angels, we are told, are seen as human infants by those approaching them from below—though this is not how they appear to themselves—because their affections are born of the union of the love of* good—*from an angel-father—and of* truth—*from an angel-mother—in conjugial love.*

And Swedenborg himself saw birds during his sojourns in the Spirit World and it was revealed to him that—in the Grand Man—rational concepts are seen as birds. Because the head corresponds to the heavens and the air. He actually experienced in his body *the fall of certain angels who had formed wrong opinions in their community about thoughts and influx—he felt a terrible tremor in his sinews and bones—and saw one dark and ugly bird and two fine and beautiful. And these solid birds were the* thoughts *of the angels, as he saw them in the world of his senses, beautiful reasonings and ugly falses. For at every level everything corresponds, from the most purely material to the most purely divine in the Divine Human.'*

*'Very strange, very strange,' said Captain
Jesse, somewhat impatiently. Himself a great
talker he could not listen passively* [. . .][15]

What I am doing here, partly, is writing my
own story, rather like the imaginings of the
characters in it. And there did happen to be a very
solid bird in the story of Emilia Tennyson Jesse.
She had a pet raven, which she kept on a kind of
leather chain, and it walked about, clonk, clonk,
clonk, on the table during the seances, and was
fed with little bits of meat, which in my story,
really annoys some of the other characters:

*Aaron the raven, perched on the arm of
the sofa, chose this moment to raise both
his wings in the air, almost clapping them,
and then to settle again, with a rattling of
his quills and various stabbing motions
of his head. He took two or three sideways
steps towards Mr Hawke, who retreated
nervously. Like many creatures who cause*

fear, Aaron seemed to be animated by
signs of anxiety. He opened his thick blue
beak and cawed, putting his head on one
side to observe the effect of this. The lids of
his eyes were also bluish and reptilian. Mrs
Jesse gave an admonitory tug on his leash.
Mr Hawke had once asked the origin of his
name, supposing it to have something to do
with Moses' brother, the High Priest who wore
the god-designed bells and pomegranates.
But Jesse replied that he was named for the
Moor in Titus Andronicus, *a play of which*
Mr Hawke had no knowledge, not having
the Tennysons' erudition. 'A sable creature,
rejoicing in his blackness, Mr Hawke,' she had
said, shortly. Mr Hawke had said that ravens
were generally birds of ill omen, he believed.
Noah's raven, in Swedenborg's interpretation
of the Word, had represented the wayward
mind wandering over an ocean of falses.
'Gross and impenetrable falsities,' he said,
looking at Aaron, 'are described in the Word

*by owls and ravens. By owls because they
live in the darkness of the night, by ravens
because they are black, as in* Isaiah *34,11,
"the owl also and the raven shall dwell in it".'*

*'Owls and ravens are God's creatures,'
Mrs Jesse replied on that occasion with some
spirit. 'I cannot believe that anything so
delightful and soft and surprised as an
owl can be a creature of evil, Mr Hawke.
Look at the screech-owls who cried back to
Wordsworth's Boy, and his mimic hootings.
My own brother Alfred was most successful
in that line as a boy, he could imitate any
bird, and had a whole family of owls who
came to his fingertips for food when he
called, and one who became a member of
our household and travelled about on his
head. He had a room under the roof of the
Rectory, under the gable.' Her face softened
at the thought of Somersby as it always did.
She took out a little leather bag and offered
the raven a small scrap of what looked like*

liver, which he took with another quick stab, tossed, turned, and swallowed. Mrs Papagay was fascinated by Mrs Jesse's scraps of flesh. She had seen her covertly put away the remnants of the roast meat from the dinner table into her pouch for the bird. There was something unsavoury about Mrs Jesse, as well, of course, as something pure and tragic. Sitting there with the staring bird and the sharp-toothed, bulge-headed monstrous little grey dog, she was like a weathered, watching head between gargoyles on a church roof, Mrs Papagay momentarily thought, over which centuries of wind and rain had swept as it stared, fretted and steadfast, out to the distance. [16]

So then they have a seance and try to call up Arthur Hallam, but don't. And finally—and this is where I feel a bit doubtful—what I would like to say about what I'm doing, is that this piece of writing is thick with very solid things, half of which are real—the raven really was real, and the bits of meat really were real—and half of which are images in the head of Swedenborg, or the people there. The feeling I wanted to get from the writing was to keep changing key, from the real, to the banal, to the terrifying, to the symbolic, to the visionary and out again, which is the feeling I get from reading about nineteenth-century spiritualism, and the feeling I get also from reading Balzac. It's a very nice kind of thing to write. I'll read you a tiny bit about the time when Sophy Sheekhy really does see a sort of creature from beyond.

'There is something in the room,' Sophy Sheekhy announced dreamily. 'Between the sofa and the window. A living creature.'

All looked towards this dark corner—those opposite Sophy Sheekhy, especially Emily Jesse, who was directly opposite her, turning their heads and craning their necks, seeing only the dim outlines of Mr Morris's pomegranates and birds and lilies.

'Can you see it clearly?' asked Mrs Papagay. 'Is it a spirit?'

'I can see it clearly. I don't know what it is. I can describe it. Up to a point. A lot of the colours don't have names.'

'Describe it.'

*'It is made up of some substance which has the appearance of——I don't know how to say this——of——*plaited glass. *Of quills, or hollow tubes of glass all bound together like plaits of hair or those pictures you see of the muscles of flayed men all woven together——but these are like molten glass. It appears to be very hot, it gives off a kind of bright* fizzing *sort of light. It is somewhat the shape of a huge decanter or flask, but it is a living creature. It has flaming eyes on the sides of a high glassy sort of head, and it has a long, long beak——or proboscis——its long neck is slightly bent and its nose or beak or proboscis——is tucked into its——into the plaits of——what in a way is its fiery breast. And it is all eyes, all golden eyes,*

inside . . . *it has in a way plumes, in three,
in three layers, all colours—I can't do the
colours—it has plumes like a great mist, a
ruff under its—head—and a kind of cloak
round its centre—and I don't know if it has a
train or a tail or winged feet, I can't* see, *it's all
stirring about all the time, and shining and
sparking and throwing off bits of light and I
get the feeling, the sensation, it doesn't like me
to describe it in demeaning human words
and comparisons—it didn't like me saying
"decanter or flask", I felt its anger, which was
hot. It does wish me to describe it, I can tell.'*

'*Is it hostile?' asked Captain Jesse.*

'*No,' said Sophy Sheekhy, slowly. She added,
'It is irritable.'*

'*Skirted his loins and thighs with downie
Gold/ And colours dipt in Heav'n,' said Mrs
Jesse.*

'*Can you see it too?' said Sophy Sheekhy.*

'*No. I was quoting the description of the
Archangel Raphael in* Paradise Lost.' [17]

The interesting thing about this, from the point of view of my own interest in writing, is that I wrote it, I saw it, but it wasn't there. Writing is a bit like seeing things that aren't there. Sophy does, in fact——alone, and not in the group——raise up the spirit of Arthur Henry Hallam. And this is a dangerous thing to write. She is accustomed to standing in her room, in front of a mirror, reciting poems——which actually I do see, I do see poems as the ghosts of dead poets——and she starts by reciting Dante Gabriel Rossetti's poem about the Blessed Virgin, the virgin in heaven, leaning over and looking for her lover, which I won't read. [18] But I'll read you the next bit:

> *Sophy Sheekhy's arms were wrapped about*
> *herself and she was swaying slightly, like*
> *a lily on its stalk, like a snake before the*
> *charmer, back and forth, her hair lifting*
> *and slipping on her shoulders. Her voice*
> *was low and pure and clear. As she spoke,*
> *she saw the thin flames, the moon curled*

*like a feather, and felt herself spinning away
from herself, as sometimes happened, as
though she had applied her huge eye to the
orifice of a great kaleidoscope where her face
whirled like a speck of tinsel amongst the
feathery flakes, snow-crystals, worlds. She
heard herself saying, as though in answer*

*'He will not come,' she said. / She wept, 'I am
aweary, aweary, / O God, that I were dead.'*

*That was another poem entirely. Reciting
that made her cold all over. She held tighter
to herself for comfort, cold breast on cold
ledge of arms, little fingers clasping at
her ribs. She was sure, almost sure, sure,
that something else breathed amongst the
floating feathers behind her. Poems rustled
together like voices. She felt a stab of pain,
like an icicle between the clutched ribs. She
heard the rattle of hail, or rain, suddenly
in great gusts on the windowpane, like*

*scattered seed. She felt a sudden weight in
the room, a heavy space, as one feels tapping
at the door of a house, knowing in advance
that it is inhabited, before the foot is heard
on the stair, the rustle and clink in the hall.
She knew she must not look behind her, and
knowing that, began drowsily to hum in her
head the richness of 'The Eve of St Agnes':*

*Out went the taper as she hurried in; / Its
little smoke, in pallid moonshine, died:
/ She clos'd the door, she panted, all akin
/ To spirits of the air, and visions wide:
/ No uttered syllable, or, woe betide! /
But to her heart, her heart was voluble, /
Paining with eloquence her balmy side; /
As though a tongueless nightingale should
swell / Her throat in vain, and die, heart-
stifled, in her dell.*

*Whatever was behind her sighed, and then
drew in its breath, with difficulty. Sophy*

Sheekhy told him dubiously, 'I think you are there. I should like to see you.'

'Perhaps you wouldn't like what you saw,' she heard, or thought she heard.

'Was that you?'

'I said, perhaps you wouldn't like what you saw.'

'It isn't my habit to like or dislike,' she found herself answering.

She took her candle and held it up to the mirror, still filled with the superstitious sense, like those poetic ladies, Madeline, the Lady of Shalott, that she must not look away from the plane of glass. The candle caused a local shimmer and gloom in the depths in which she thought she saw something move.

'We cannot always help ourselves as to that,' he said, much more clearly.

'Please——' she breathed to the glass.

She felt him move in on her, closer, closer. She heard the words of the poem spoken in an ironic, slightly harsh voice.

*Into her dream he melted, as the rose /
Blendeth its odour with the violet, — /
Solution sweet:*

*Her hands shook, the face behind
her bulged and tightened, sagged and
reassembled, not pale, but purple-veined,
with staring blue eyes and parched thin lips,
above a tremulous chin. There was a sudden
gust of odour, not rose, not violet, but earth-
mould and corruption.*

*'You see,' said the harsh, small voice. 'I am
a dead man, you see.'*

*Sophy Sheekhy took a breath and turned
round. She saw her own little white bed,
and a row of doves preening themselves on
the cast-iron bedstead. She saw, briefly, a
parrot, scarlet and blue, on the windowsill.
She saw dark glass, and she saw him,
struggling, it seemed to her, to keep his
appearance, his sort-of-substance, together,
with a kind of deadly defiance.*

She knew immediately that he was the man. Not because she recognised him, but because she did not, and yet he fitted the descriptions, the curls, the thin mouth, the bar on the brow. He wore an ancient high-collared shirt, out of fashion when Sophy's mother was a small child, and stained breeches. He stood there, trembling and morose. The trembling was not exactly human. It caused his body to swell and contract as though sucked out of shape and pressed back into it. Sophy took a few steps towards him. She saw that his brows and lashes were caked with clay. He said again, 'I am a dead man.'

He moved away from her, walking like someone finding his feet after a long illness, and sat down on the seat in the window, displacing a number of white birds, who ran fluttering and resettled at the foot of the curtains. Sophy followed him, and stood and considered him. He was very young.

*His lovers on earth watched and waited for
him like some wise god gone before, but
this young man was younger than she was
herself, and seemed to be in the last stages of
exhaustion, owing to his state. She had been
told, in the Church of the New Jerusalem,
of Swedenborg's encounters with the newly
dead, who refused to believe that they were
dead, who attended their own funerals
with indignant interest. Later, Swedenborg
taught, the dead, who took with them into
the next world the affections and minds
of this terrestrial space, had to find their
true selves and their true, their appropriate
companions, amongst spirits and angels.
They had to learn that they were dead, and
then to go on. She said, 'How is it with you?
What is your state?'*

'As you see me. Baffled and impotent.'

*'You are much mourned, much missed.
More than any being I know.'*

A spasm of anguish twisted the dull red

*face, and Sophy Sheekhy suddenly felt in her
blood and bones that the mourning was
painful to him. It dragged him down, or
back, or under. He moved his heavy tongue
in his mouth, unaccustomed now.*

*'I walk. Between. Outside. I cannot tell
you. I am part of nothing. Impotent and
baffled,' he added, quick and articulate
suddenly, as though these were words he
knew, had tamed doggedly in his mind over
the long years. Which might not, of course,
appear to him to be years. A thousand ages
in thy sight are but an instant gone. She
spoke from her heart.*

'You are so young.*'*

'I am young. And dead.'

'And not forgotten.'

Again, the same spasm of pain.

'And alone.' The pure self-pity of the young.

'I would like to help you, if I could.'

It was help he appeared to need. [19]

Now I'll read a passage near the end. This is the scene in which the people at the seance do manage, in some sort of way, to rouse up the conjugial angel, or some such presence. Mrs Papagay starts by doing automatic writing, and this activity lies somewhere between being a fraud and being inspired by something. She wrote:

> Blessed are they that mourn / For THEY SHALL BE COMFORTED.

> *'Is anyone there?' Mr Hawke enquired. 'Any message for any particular person present?'*

> He will not come, she said.

> *'Who will not come?' said Mr Hawke.*
> *'Arthur,' said Mrs Jesse, with a little sigh.*
> *'It means Arthur, I am sure.'*
> *The pen wrote rapidly.*

> And he that shuts Love out in turn shall be

/ Shut out from Love and on her threshold
lie / Howling in outer darkness.

*The pen appeared to like this word, for it
played with it, repeating it several times,
'howling', 'howling', 'howling', and then
adding*

those that lawless and incertain thoughts
Imagine howling——'tis too horrible . . .

*'A poetic spirit,' said Mr Hawke.
'The first two are Alfred,' said Mrs Jesse.
'The pen may have hooked them, so to
speak, out of my mind. The last is from*
Measure for Measure, *a passage about the
fate of the soul after death which Alfred was
much struck by, as we all were. I have no
idea who is uttering these things.'* [. . .]

*Sophy felt cold hands at her neck, cold
fingers on her warm lips. The flesh crept over
the bones of her skull, along the backs of her*

fingers, under the whalebone. She began to shake and jerk. She fell back open-mouthed in her chair and saw something, someone, standing in the bay of the window. It was larger than life, and more exiguous, a kind of pillar of smoke, or fire or cloud, in a not exactly human form. It was not the dead young man, for whom she had felt such pity, it was a living creature with three wings, all hanging loosely on one side of it. On that side, the winged side, it was dull gold and had the face of a bird of prey, dignified, golden-eyed, feather-breasted, powdered with hot metallic particles. On its other side, turned into the shadow, it was grey like wet clay, and formless, putting out stumps that were not arms, moving what was not a mouth in a thin whisper. It spoke in low voices, one musical, one a papery squeak. 'Tell her I wait.'

'Tell whom?' said Sophy, in a small voice they all heard.

*'Emilia. I triumph in conclusive bliss.
Tell her. We shall be joined and made one
Angel.'*

*It was hungry for the life of the living
creatures in the room.*

*'Sophy,' said Mrs Papagay. 'What do you
see?'*

*'Gold wings,' said Sophy. 'It says, "I wait."
It says to tell you, "I triumph in conclusive
bliss." It says to tell Emily——Mrs Jesse——
Emily——that——they shall be joined, and
made one Angel. In the hereafter, that is.'*

*Emily Jesse gave a great sigh. She let go
Sophy's cold hand, and detached Sophy's
other hand from her husband's, breaking
the circle. Sophy lay inert, like a prisoner
before an inquisitor, staring at the half-
angel, whom no one else saw, or really
felt the presence of, and Emily Jesse put her
hand into her husband's.*

*'Well, Richard,' she said. 'We may not
always have got on together as well as we*

should, and our marriage may not have been a success, but I consider that an extremely unfair arrangement, and shall have nothing to do with it. We have been through bad times in this world, and I consider it only decent to share out good times, presuming we have them, in the next.' [20]

Now this is an exact quote from Emilia Tennyson Jesse, this is what she did say when she was told they would be made one angel.

Richard picked up her hand and looked at it.
'Why Emily,' he said, and then again, 'why, Emily——'
'You are not usually at a loss for words,' said his wife.
'No, I am not. It is only that——I understood——I understood you to be waiting——for some such communication. I had never supposed you would say——

anything like—what you have just said.'

'It may be that you have other ideas,' said Mrs Jesse.

'You know that *is not so. I have tried to be understanding, I have tried to be patient, I have respected—'*

'Too well, too well, you tried too well, we both—'

Captain Jesse shook his head, like a surfacing swimmer.

'But all through these séances I understood you to be waiting—'

'I do love him,' said Emily. 'It is hard to love the dead. It is hard to love the dead enough.' [21]

Finally, I would like to read a paragraph about things in this earth, which, to a novelist, are miraculous just because they exist. They all have tea. Mrs Jesse

poured tea. The oil-lamps cast a warm light on the teatray. The teapot was china, with little

*roses painted all over it, crimson and blush-
pink and celestial blue, and the cups were
garlanded with the same flowers. There were
sugared biscuits, each with a flower made
out of piped icing, creamy, violet, snow-white.
Sophy Sheekhy watched the stream of topaz-
coloured liquid fall from the spout, steaming
and aromatic. This too was a miracle, that
gold-skinned persons in China and bronze-
skinned persons in India should gather leaves
which should come across the seas safely in
white-winged ships, encased in lead, encased
in wood, surviving storms and whirlwinds,
sailing on under hot sun and cold moon,
and come here, and be poured from bone-
china, made from fine clay, moulded by
clever fingers, in the Pottery Towns, baked in
kilns, glazed with slippery shiny clay, baked
again, painted with rosebuds by artist-hands
holding fine, fine, brushes, delicately turning
the potter's wheel and implanting, with a kiss
of sable-hairs, floating buds on an azure*

*ground, or a dead white ground, and that
sugar should be fetched from where black
men and women slaved and died terribly to
make these delicate flowers that melted on the
tongue like scrolls in the mouth of the Prophet
Isaiah, that flour should be milled, and milk
shaken into butter, and both worked together
into these momentary delights, baked in Mrs
Jesse's oven and piled elegantly on to a plate
to be offered to Captain Jesse with his wool-
white head and smiling eyes, to Mrs Papagay,
flushed and agitated, to her sick self, and the
black bird and the dribbling Pug, in front of
the hot coals of fire, in the benign lamplight.
Any of them might so easily not have been there
to drink tea, or eat the sweetmeats. Storms and
ice-floes might have taken Captain Jesse, grief
or childbearing might have destroyed his wife,
Mrs Papagay might have lapsed into penury
and she herself have died as an overworked
servant, but here they were and their eyes were
bright and their tongues tasted goodness.* [21]

Q: *Can I begin by asking a question about the idea of a soulmate? Do you think we have someone who is our other half? And to what extent did people believe this to be so during the nineteenth century? Or is this something the story was aiming to criticize?*

A: Since I was talking about cake, I was having my cake and eating it really. I am very worried, I think, by the idea of the conjugial angel, and everybody having only one partner. I was terribly distressed that poor Emilia Tennyson was required by her religion to wait forever for Arthur Henry Hallam, who had been so long dead. And of course, there is an irony. I didn't read the whole story, but in many ways, if Henry Hallam had a soulmate it was Alfred Tennyson, who mourned him and wrote some wonderful verse. I thought I was going to read out the section about the two souls being one together and flying to the heavens. But I was also saying that even if Captain Jesse wasn't Mrs Jesse's soulmate, they were happy, in a way. I wasn't able to read all the bits of Captain Jesse talking endlessly. And of course, if you knew him it would be infuriating, but if you are reading a novel it is quite interesting. I think I don't believe in soulmates, but I think that some people find them.

Q: *I would like to ask a question about your interest in the way mediums collect information. You were talking about the different ways in which this information comes, i.e., in the form of visions or words. I wondered if you had, in your own experience, moved further and recognized the information as*

*coming from somewhere else, say a divine
source, or is it a material access of information
that only appears to be from somewhere else?*

A: I think I am using both the experience of Mrs
Papagay and Sophy Sheekhy as metaphors for
the novelist. The story says that Mrs Papagay is
a novelist, and her mind works like a novelist.
There are several places where she does what
we all do, just like every ordinary human being,
without spiritual content: we look at people and
we start imagining their lives . . . and she can't
stop herself, for instance, imagining how on earth
Mrs Hearnshaw manages to become pregnant
for a sixth time when she had lost five children
in a row, and was in such a state of distress. Mrs
Papagay's imagination starts sagging, as it were,
and that isn't anything to do with the divine, it's
just human. You look at somebody and you start
making a story for them and you pick up signs
that they give you, about something they tell you,
and you think there is a short story in that, or there

is a big novel in that. That's part of what I was doing. I don't have any God, so if you say 'divine', that's where I stop. But 'visionary' I don't stop at.

There are writers who see things that aren't there, and occasionally I see things that aren't there. I can look at that last half-angel, which is dead on one side, and I can, in my mind—which is what you were talking about—look at it from more angles the more I see. I know what sort of structure it is, I keep looking and can see whether it's moving or not. I think I simply see that as one reason why human beings make works of art. I stay there. And works of art do that to me.

But Balzac, I think—and I haven't got to the end of Balzac's relationship with Swedenborg— thought that the novel was the divine human, which is to say that any novel, as it were, is a whole world, and this is the divine human. And this is penetrated from outside by the spirit. He thought that language was a way in which that world interpenetrated our world, and he thought language was both material and spiritual. He has a novel in his head, and a novel out there, and I want to write about that, because if you are writing a novel, all sorts of solid things are in there and you project them out. Then once you have seen them, they are out. And this is about as far as I can go. Balzac goes wildly off into spiritual theories about angels and things, but he has some very beautiful spiritual theories about language as a medium, which I find increasingly interesting. That is, I'm interested myself, on the very edges—not in the middle—of all this.

Q: *I would like to ask whether the connection between* Morpho Eugenia *and* The Conjugial Angel *was pragmatic, that is, were they written at the same time? I am referring in particular to the quite shocking ending of* Morpho Eugenia, *which feels very different to* The Conjugial Angel.

A: I think the link is to do with teaching nineteenth-century fiction and poetry, really. I felt

that the whole period could . . . having worked
on the seventeenth century, which presented
a Christian structure to thought, even if one
didn't agree with it . . . and *Morpho Eugenia* is
about what there is in the absence of a Christian
structure, and this structure is Darwinian. And
also the structure of the world of Sir Walter Scott.
Nobody picked it up, but all the white alabasters
have names like Walter Scott Saxons. And William
and Matilda are the invading Normans. So it is
a kind of Victorian historical novel about the
inevitable progress of the stronger people—and
the aristocrats are the ones dying out. In this
sense it is not a religious story at all, and all the
imagery about the ants is an analogy of the slave-
making races of human beings.

At the same time, at that turn of the nineteenth
century, people performed these works of art.
There was an attempt, which Swedenborg was
central to I think, to make a religious structure
of the world, to make a religious vision of things,
so these two stories are two sides of the diptych

really. One side is Darwinian, and I know bits of
it are terrible, but it ends quite hopefully, with
them sailing off in the ship with Mrs Papagay's
husband taking them back to South America.
And *The Conjugial Angel* ends hopefully too. In a
sense I see them both as comic. In *The Conjugial
Angel* I wanted to go back to making an object,
to making a little world in which real visions
of teacups and spiritual visions of transparent
angels were completely part of one material
imagined thing. So it was the other side that isn't
Darwinism at all.

Q: *Is the idea that you have two beings fused
into one from Plato's* Symposium *or is it from
Swedenborg, with a glance of Balzac?*

A: I think it is both. I also think there are feminist
arguments against the way Swedenborg presents
the female half of the angel, whereas in Plato,
it could almost be two men. But I think this is a
recurrent idea throughout human thought, that

we are somehow incomplete and need somebody else to be our other half.

Balzac in *Séraphîta* has a double-sexed being who is seen by the young woman in the story as a young man, and whom the young man in the story sees as a woman, and who is flirting with him rather appallingly. This being ascends to heaven and gets loved, as any other kind of human thing, and becomes lost in the love of God and it ceases to be. . . it sort of leaves us. I think it is interesting because at the banal level in novels, this idea of the perfect other half—and I've come to this conclusion—is often quite felicitous, you ought to look at people as they are. I got terribly attached to Captain Jesse who is both immensely heroic and immensely tiresome. I think it would be [difficult to be] anybody's other half, but it would be rather wonderful to live with him.

Q: *Much of* The Conjugial Angel *appears to draw on* Heaven and Hell, *which is Swedenborg's best-known book. In it he describes, in some detail, his ideas of the next life and the spiritual world, etc. But* Heaven and Hell *also has a strange beginning, in which the first chapter, or the first four pages, are quite different from the rest of the book because he begins by describing the God of Heaven.* [22] *Christians believe that there are three divine persons but Swedenborg rejects this saying that there is only one. He also says a lot about when first arriving in the spiritual world—which is what everybody wants to know, i.e., what happens when I die, what happens when I wake up?—but the first chapter seems to me very important because it raises the question 'who is the God of Heaven'? There is something here that is often missed.*

A: I missed it too. I stop at God. I'm not very good at writing believers either, except sideways, if they have intimations of immortality.

Q: *One of the interesting things about Swedenborg is that he had these visions going on all the time, with a tremendous amount of information coming in.*

A: Yes, and this is why I love him so, because he is so precise and so endlessly capable of describing whatever it is was he was experiencing. I love the bit about how he knows exactly what dead people feel like. He knows that they have to go to their own funeral and they are complaining because they don't think that they are dead. He's met them. They tell him. He's a sort of gift for a fiction writer, because it is given as fact and in this way he's not like anyone else. And for the Victorians he was a scientist, a doubter, a real materialist— living with real material sciences—he was somehow authenticated with the things he saw.

Q: *On the question of inspiration, do you ever read something back and think, 'I didn't realize I'd written that'? And is there ever a case when it feels like automatic writing, when you look back at something and think, 'was that really there?'*

A: I think we all do. I don't reread anything I write, I try to go on and write another thing. I think mostly about the thing in my head, which isn't yet formed, that hasn't got a shape. So if you find yourself reading something, reading out aloud, something you wrote a long time ago, you do so for a slightly peculiar reason: which coming here is for me because my relation with Swedenborg is peculiar. I did think, once or twice, 'did I write that?', yes, but I don't think it was because it was dictated to me or anything. I think it was just that it is not your conscious self that writes everything.

Q: *I am very interested in your comments about Balzac, and in particular his short novellas,* Séraphîta *and* Louis Lambert. *I remember, as an undergraduate, preparing for my final dissertation and visiting a Balzacian scholar in London. I had travelled all the way from Nottingham to seek guidance on how he thought these works fitted into*

Balzac's La Comédie humaine. *Anyway, as
soon as the scholar realized I was interested in*
Séraphîta *and* Louis Lambert *he rather dimissed
me and those works as being, in some way,
inauthentic, or an aberration. I would
therefore be very interested to know what you
are working on and whether your research
draws upon these two works.*

A: I'm giving a lecture on Saturday in memory
of Malcom Bowie, who was Professor of French
at Cambridge. [23] And this is a lecture about a sort
of line that goes through from Dante, to Balzac,
to *Middlemarch* and it is, in a sense, about the
religious structure of the realist novel. Because
I hadn't realized until I was writing an article
for an Italian newspaper that *Middlemarch*
is a translation of the first line of the *Divine
Comedy*—'Nel mezzo del cammin di nostra
vita'—the middle of the march of our life. Then
I started working out a lot of things about the
shape of Balzac, and its influence on George

Eliot. Of course, she almost never refers to it, because she felt he was too obscene and it wasn't respectable to refer to him. And I've always been interested in the visionary side of Balzac, which I think shapes his theories of the nature of fiction and of the solidity in language.

So I went back to reading *Séraphîta,* although most of what I am talking about in fact is from *Illusions perdues*. And another thing I will say is that for some years when I was a teacher at UCL, I used to be an external examiner on the East Anglia Creative Writing MA in fiction, and there was a religious belief that Balzac thought the world was just like a series of square bricks. They all produced the same metaphor, and I've never been sure where they got it from. They assumed that Balzac thought that everything was materialistic and viewed the work as a kind of nineteenth-century journalism. They had no idea that works such as *Séraphîta* existed and that Balzac was an overall visionary. But it's not just *Séraphîta*, it crops up all over in Balzac. So yes, you are reading him wrongly if you aren't aware of all of this.

Q: *I really want to ask you something about literary form, because you said something about Keats and you talk about Balzac's novels as these divine visionary formations. You put wonderful synthesized poems into your novel* Possession, *and you've played with literary form, but you said earlier this evening that poems were ghosts of dead poets. Is there some way that novels are ghosts of dead novelists, is there a hierarchy?*

A: That is very interesting because I don't think *Middlemarch* is the ghost of George Eliot whereas I do think of 'Mr Sludge, "The Medium"', for instance, as the voice of Browning.[24] It's partly to do with the work of art as a thing. A poem is its rhythm. And although a novel has rhythm, you would have to be terribly, terribly clever to create a rhythm for the whole work. And even if you achieve this, you would have lost your novel.

Q: *Is that true of Virginia Woolf?*

A: I'm not happy with Virginia Woolf.

Q: *'Mr Sludge, "The Medium"' is a poem about Daniel Dunglas Home, who was a friend of J J G Wilkinson. The Swedenborg Society was very impressed with Home at one point. William Wilkinson, his brother, was a former Secretary of the Swedenborg Society, and he ghosted Home's memoirs. So there is a direct connection here. Anyway, my question is this: had you written when Elizabeth Browning was still alive, would she have been upset?* [25]

A: She would have been very upset. I was once giving a lecture on Robert Browning and Elizabeth Barrett Browning in Texas, and I wrote on Robert Browning's images and use of metaphors. He used very concrete, elegant little metaphors—and that was a very interesting thing to do, but no, poems are ghosts, they are both more separate, and more a part of the person. 'The Eve of St. Agnes' is the ghost of Keats.[26] But I don't feel the presence of George Eliot when I'm reading *Middlemarch*, except when she says: 'If we had a keen vision and feeling of all ordinary human life, it would be like hearing the grass grow and the squirrel's heart beat, and we should die of that roar which lies on the other side of silence'.[27] That was her ghost. The novel is a material thing, as Balzac would have hastened to point out, and a poem sits in your head with no material thing, and that's part of it as well, it gets inside your brain and haunts you.

Endnotes

1   See F R Leavis, *The Great Tradition: George Eliot,
    Henry James, Joseph Conrad* (New York: George W
    Stewart, 1950), p. 128 and *The Common Pursuit*
    (New York: New York University Press, 1964), p. 224.
    Leavis is citing Quentin Anderson, 'Henry James and the
    New Jerusalem', in *The Kenyon Review*, vol. 8, no. 4
    (Autumn, 1946).

2   Henry James, Sr, *The Secret of Swedenborg: Being an
    Elucidation of his Doctrine of the Divine Natural
    Humanity* (Boston: Fields, Osgood & Co., 1869).

3   Emerson is doubtful as the source of the quip. It has
    previously been attributed to William Dean Howells as
    cited in a letter by Charles Eliot Norton dated 11 June
    1907. See Sara Norton and M A DeWolfe Howe, *Letters
    of Charles Eliot Norton with Biographical Comment*,
    2 vols. (Boston and New York: Houghton Mifflin
    Company, 1913), vol. II, p. 379.

4   Henry James, *The Bostonians: A Novel* (London and
    New York: Macmillan and Co., 1886).

5   Iris Murdoch, *The Time of the Angels* (London: Chatto
    & Windus, 1966), p. 171.

6   Henry James, *The Bostonians*, p. 5.

7   Henry James, *The Golden Bowl*, 2 vols. (New York:
    Charles Scribner's Sons, 1904).

8   Honoré de Balzac, 'Introduction', in *The Wild Ass' Skin
    and other stories*, tr. Ellen Marriage (Philadelphia:
    The Gebbie Publishing Co., 1898), p. xlvii. Balzac's
    'avant-propos' to *La Comédie humaine* was first
    published in 1842.

9   Balzac's *Séraphîta* was first published in *Revue de
    Paris* in June and July 1834 before being issued as the
    second volume of *Le livre mystique* (Paris: Werdet,
    1835). *Les Proscrits* and *Louis Lambert* formed the
    first volume of *Le livre mystique*.

10 A S Byatt's *Angels and Insects* was first published in
    1992. Page references in the following notes are to the
    edition printed by Vintage in 2018.

11 Alfred Tennyson, *In Memoriam* (London: Edward
    Moxon, 1850).

12 Fryn Tennyson Jesse, letter to T H Vail Motter (1940),
    in Arthur Henry Hallam, *The Letters of Arthur
    Henry Hallam*, ed. Jack Kolb (Columbus: Ohio State
    University Press, 1981), p. 802.

13 A S Byatt, *Angels and Insects*, pp. 163-5.

14 Ibid., pp. 166-7.

15 Ibid., pp. 179-81.

16 Ibid., pp. 182-3.

17 Ibid., pp. 201-2.

18 Dante Gabriel Rossetti's 'The Blessed Damozel' was first published in the second issue of *The Germ* in 1850.

19 A S Byatt, *Angels and Insects*, pp. 248-50.

20 Ibid., pp. 282-3.

21 Ibid., pp. 283-4.

22 Emanuel Swedenborg's *De Coelo et ejus Mirabilibus, et de Inferno* was first published in London in 1758. The most recent English translation is *Heaven and Hell*, tr. K C Ryder (London: Swedenborg Society, 2010).

23 Malcolm Bowie (1943–2007), Master of Christ's College at the University of Cambridge from 2002 to 2006. A S Byatt delivered her lecture 'Balzac: The Animal, the Human, and the Form of the Novel' on Saturday 16 January 2010 at the Wilkins Gustave Tuck Lecture Theatre, University College London as part of the Malcolm Bowie Memorial Lecture Series.

24 Robert Browning, 'Mr. Sludge, "The Medium"', in *Dramatis Personae* (London: Chapman and Hall, 1864), pp. 171-236.

25 James John Garth Wilkinson (1812-99), author, homoeopathic physician and translator of Swedenborg.

William Wilkinson (1814-97), spiritualist publisher and charity campaigner, who served as Secretary of the Swedenborg Society 1842-60. Daniel Dunglas Home (1833-86), Scottish spiritualist and medium. William apparently was the ghostwriter of the first series of Home's memoirs, *Incidents in My Life* (London: Longman, Green, Longman, Roberts & Green, 1863).

26 John Keats, 'The Eve of St. Agnes', written in 1819 and first published in *Lamia, Isabella, The Eve of St. Agnes* (London: Taylor and Hessey, 1820), pp. 81-106.

27 George Eliot, *Middlemarch: A Study of Provincial Life*, 8 vols. (Edinburgh and London: William Blackwood and Sons, 1871-2), p. 351.